# Daniel Learns to Share

adapted by Becky Friedman
based on the screenplay "Daniel Shares His Tigertastic Car"
written by Wendy Harris
poses and layouts by Jason Fruchter

Ready-to-Read

Simon Spotlight
New York   London   Toronto   Sydney   New Delhi

Hi, neighbor!

I am at the park.

I am playing cars
with my friends.

*Wee-o!* O the Owl
has a police car!

Prince Wednesday
does not have a car.

I do not want him to play with my car. It is mine.

Prince Wednesday is sad.

My dad tells us
how to share.

You can take a turn, and then I will get it back.

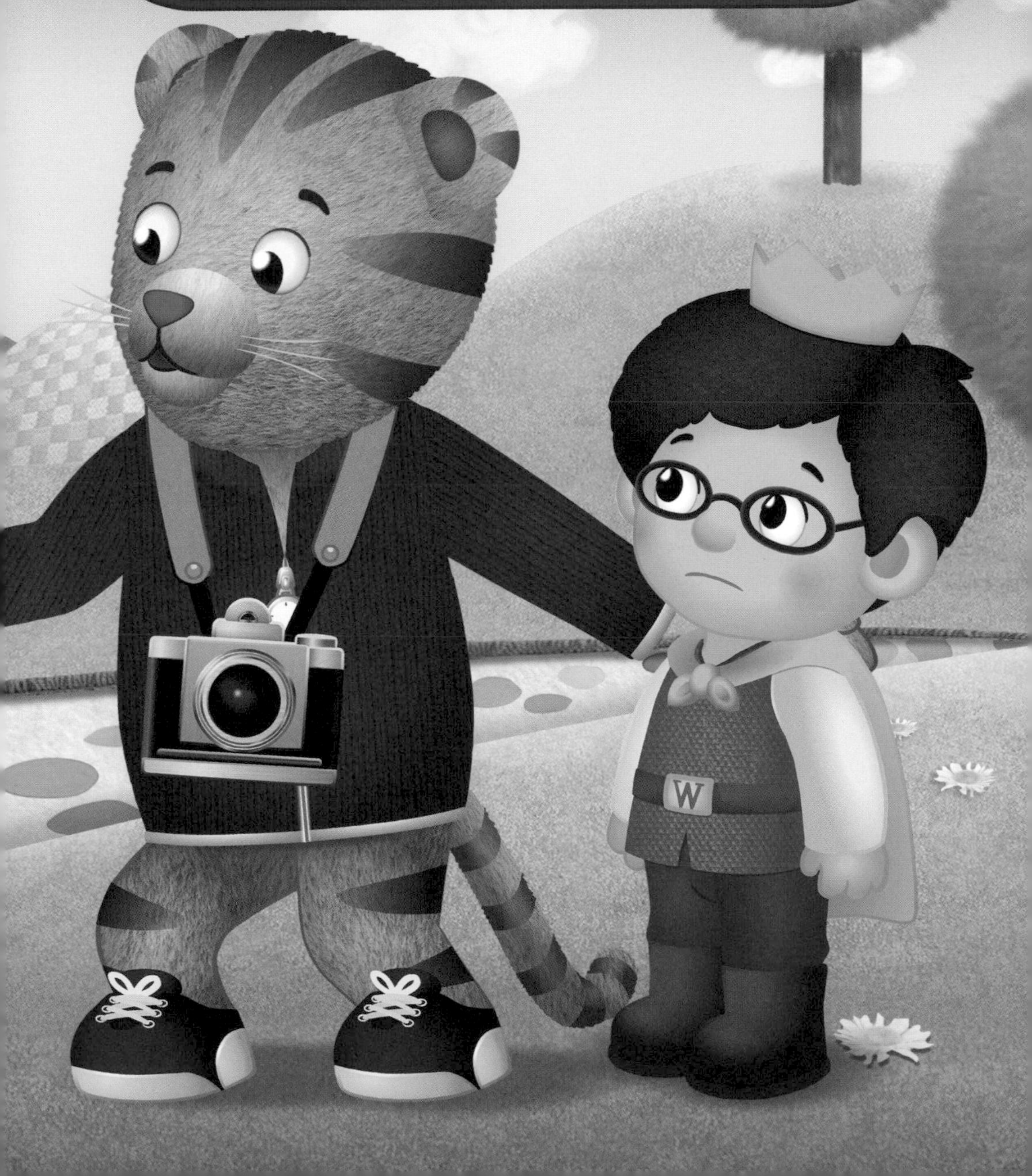

Now Prince Wednesday is happy.

My friends play with their cars.

I play too.

*Vroom! Honk! Wee-o!*

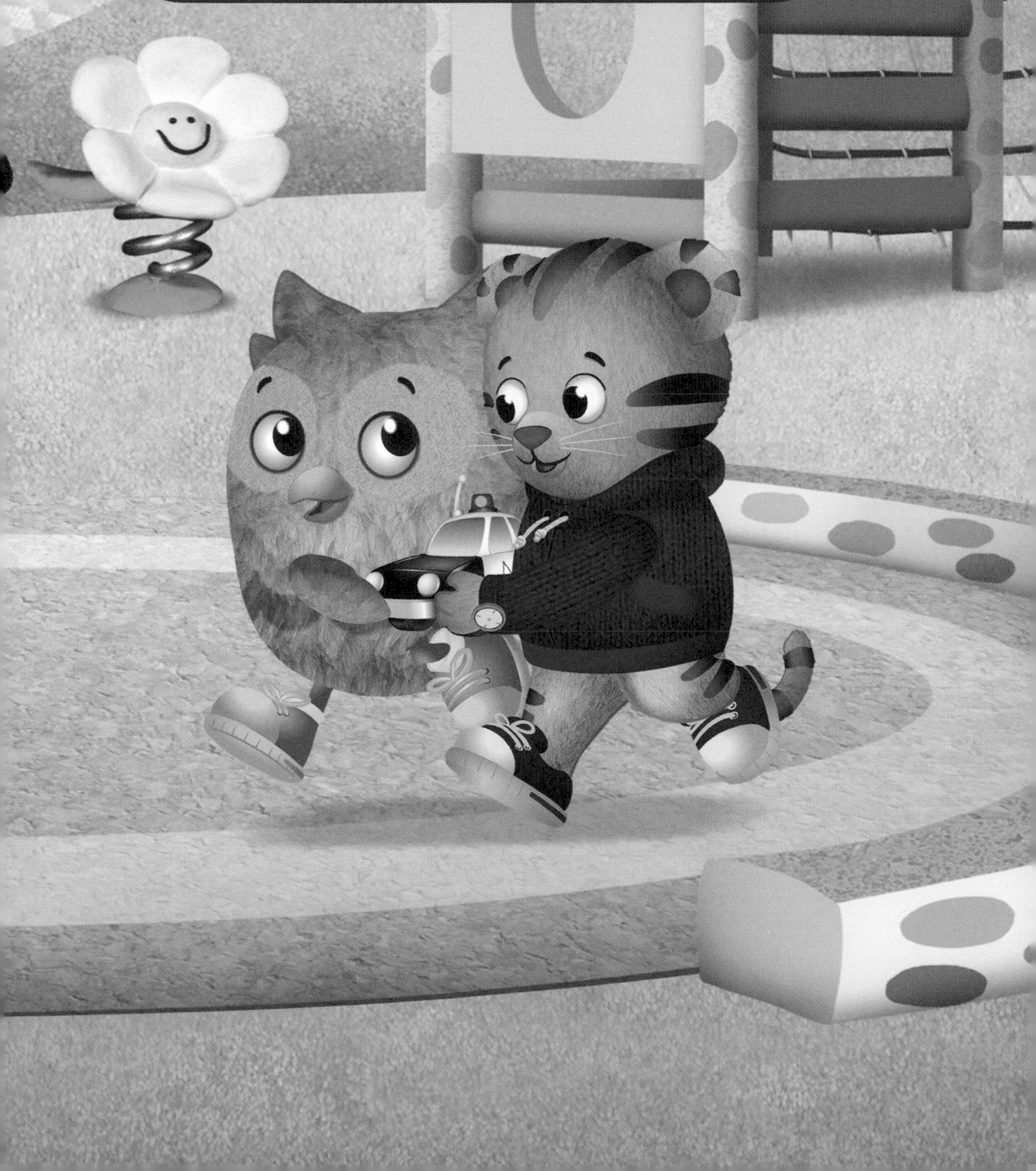

"Here is your car back," says Prince Wednesday.

"We can race our cars!" says Miss Elaina.

"You can use my car!"
says Miss Elaina.

You can take a turn, and then I will get it back.

What will Miss Elaina race with?

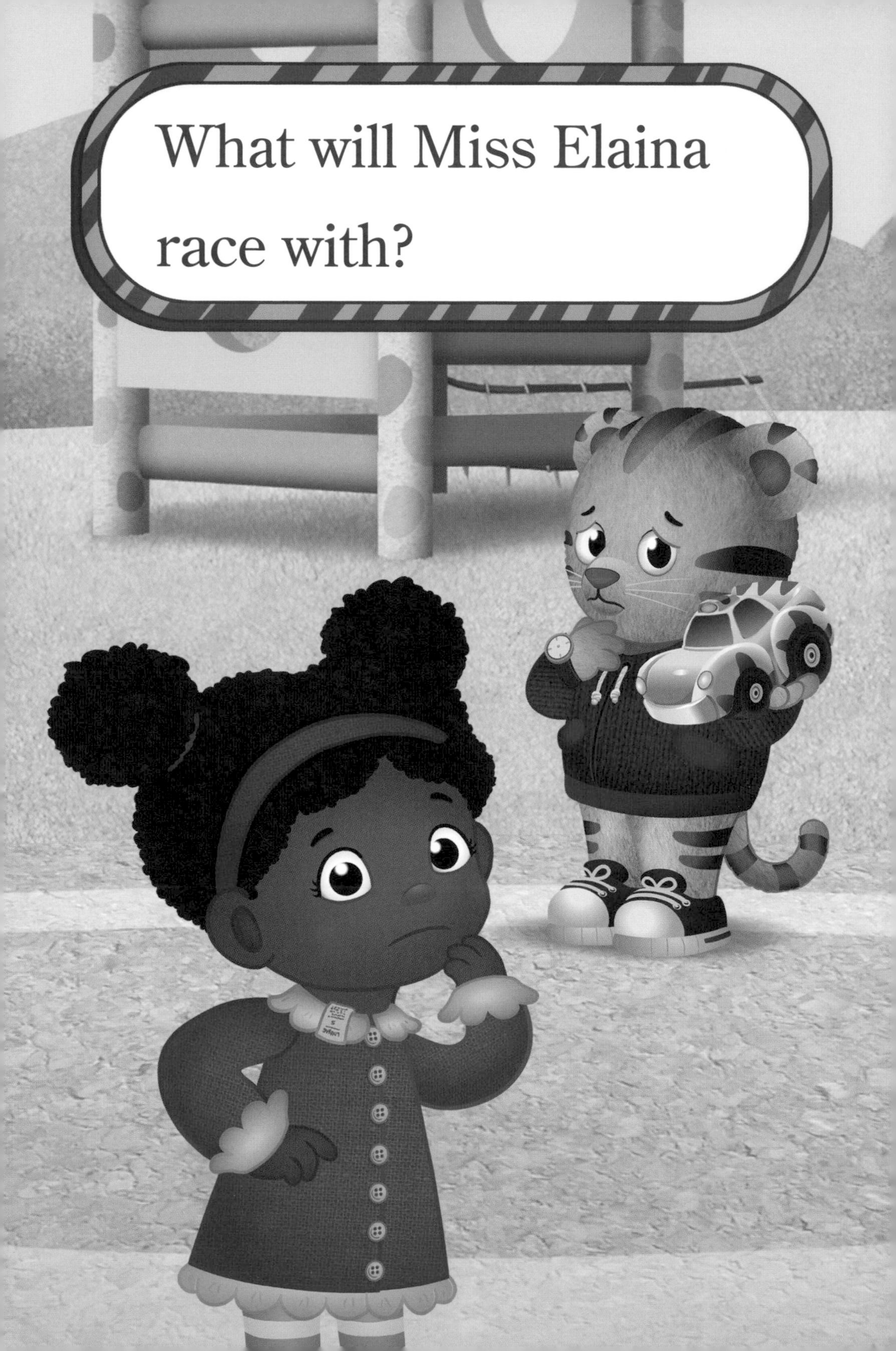

Miss Elaina uses a pretend car.

Vroom! Honk! Wee-o!

Prince Wednesday gives the truck back.

Miss Elaina is happy.

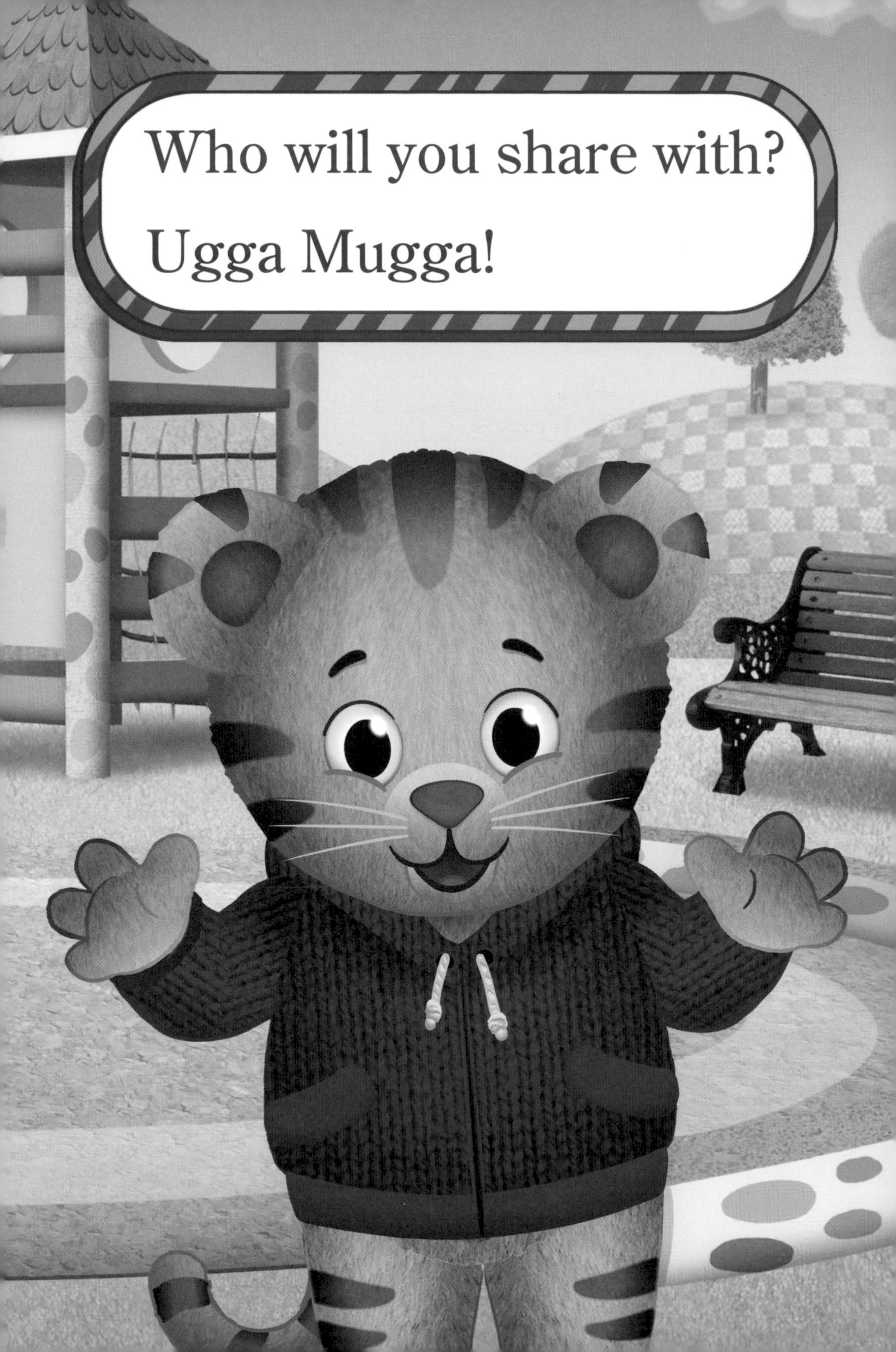
Who will you share with?
Ugga Mugga!

# Daniel Goes
# Out for Dinner

adapted by Maggie Testa

based on the screenplay "A Night Out at the Restaurant"

written by Becky Friedman

poses and layouts by Jason Fruchter

Ready-to-Read

Simon Spotlight

New York   London   Toronto   Sydney   New Delhi

Hi, neighbor!

We are going out for dinner.

I open my menu.

What food do you think looks yummy?

I want the
chicken and broccoli.

Yum!

We tell our waiter what we want to eat.

Our waiter will bring the food to the table.

Now we have to wait for our food to be cooked.

It is very, very

hard to wait.

My mom knows

what we can do.

"When you wait,
you can play, sing,
or imagine anything."

But what can we do

at the table?

"You can play a quiet,

sit-down game,"

says my dad.

"We can play 'what is missing,'" says Katerina.

Look at the things
on the table.

Katerina hides

one of the things.

# What is missing?

The salt was missing!

That was fun.
The food is
still not here.

We still have to wait.

What should we do
while we wait?

When you wait,
you can play, sing,
or imagine anything.

We can imagine that the things on the table can play with us!

We do not have to
wait anymore.

The food is here.

It is time to eat!

I am glad I waited
for my food.

It is so yummy!

I can play, sing,

or imagine anything

to make waiting easier.

# DANIEL TIGER'S NEIGHBORHOOD

# Friends
# Help Each Other

adapted by Farrah McDoogle
based on the screenplay "Friends Help Each Other" written by Wendy Harris
poses and layouts by Jason Fruchter

Ready-to-Read

Simon Spotlight
New York   London   Toronto   Sydney   New Delhi

Hi, neighbor!

Today I am playing

with Katerina Kittycat.

"Meow, Meow! Do you want to have a tea party?" asks Katerina.

That chair is heavy!
I can help!

"No, thank you," says Katerina. "I can do it all by myself."

Oh no!

Katerina bumps the table with the chair.

Everything falls on the floor!

"What happened?"
asks Henrietta Pussycat.

"I made a mess," cries Katerina. "Our tea party is ruined!"

"Maybe Daniel can help!" says Henrietta.

Friends help each other,
yes they do.

"Teatime!"
says Katerina.

"I want to pour the tea by myself!"

Oh no!

Katerina spills the tea.

I can help clean up
the tea!

Friends help each other, yes they do!

"Do you want to pour more tea?" asks Henrietta.

"Yes! But this time
I will not do it
all by myself!" says Katerina.

Yes!

*Friends help each other,
yes they do!*

I am happy I helped
my friend today!
Ugga Mugga!

# Daniel Visits the Library

adapted by Maggie Testa
based on the screenplay "Calm for Storytime"
written by Wendy Harris
poses and layouts by Jason Fruchter

Ready-to-Read

Simon Spotlight
New York   London   Toronto   Sydney   New Delhi

Hi, neighbor!
We are going to the library for storytime.

I am so excited!
Are you?

"Trolley cannot go until you are calm," says Dad.

But how can I be calm when I feel so excited?

"Try this with me," says Dad.

Give a squeeze,
nice and slow.

Take a deep breath and let it go.

"Hoo! Hoo! Hello," says O the Owl.

At last it is storytime!

X the Owl reads a book to us.

Prince Wednesday hops like a frog.

"Ribbit, ribbit," he says.

"Storytime is a time to be quiet and calm," says X the Owl.

Do you know how we can help Prince Wednesday feel calm?

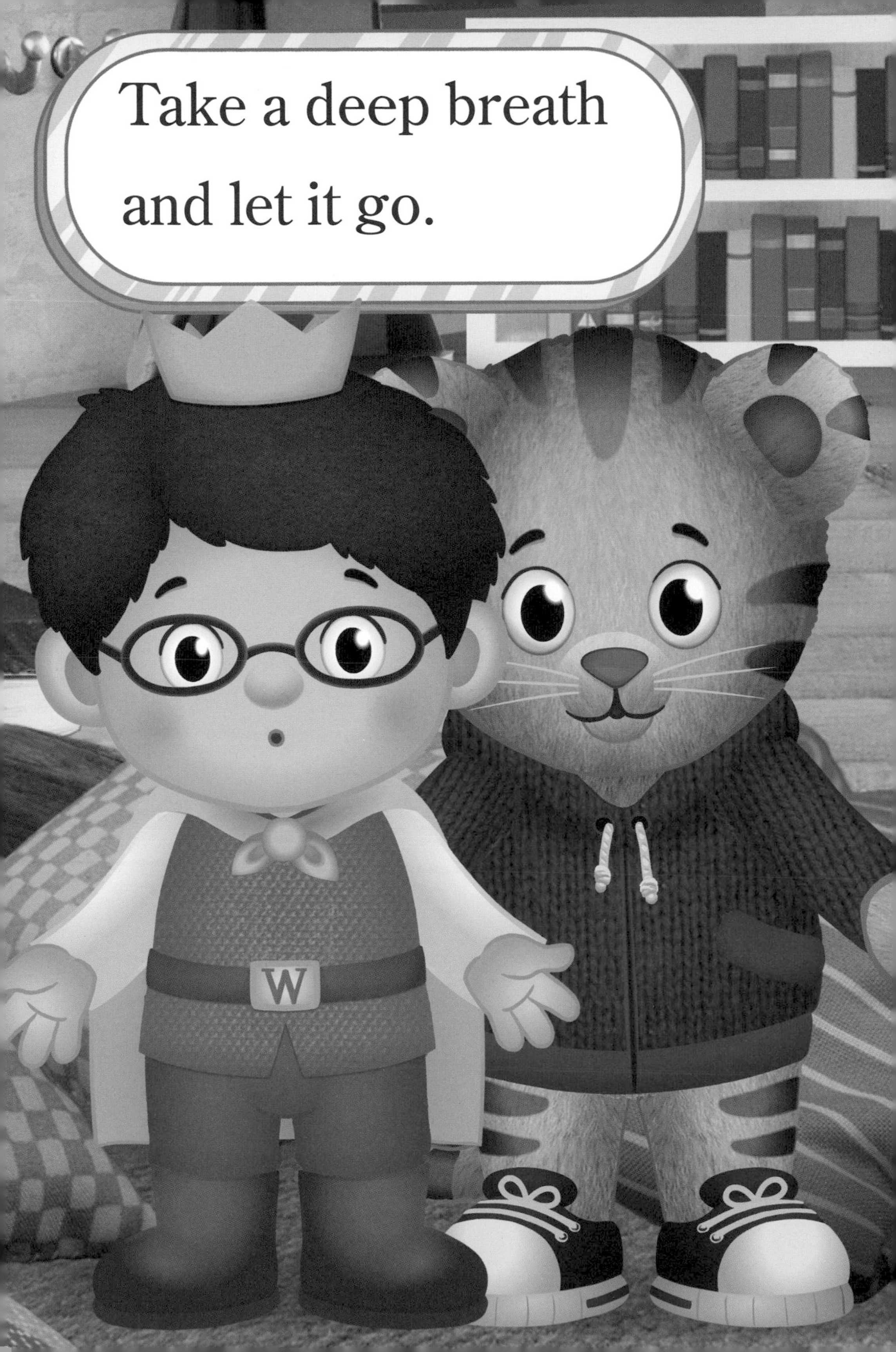
Take a deep breath and let it go.

We listen to the story.

X the Owl finishes the story.

"The end," he says.

Storytime is over. Now we can go outside and play.

Have you ever wanted to be calm when you were excited?

Next time that happens, you know what to do.